I AM READING
RICKY'S RAT GANG

To: Rees
Fr: Edan

ANTHONY MASTERS

ILLUSTRATED BY
CHRIS FISHER

KINGFISHER
BOSTON

For my daughter's very dear friends
Jacob and Isaac Pursglove—A. M.
For Joe and Will—C. F.

KINGFISHER
a Houghton Mifflin Company imprint
222 Berkeley Street
Boston, Massachusetts 02116
www.houghtonmifflinbooks.com

First published by Kingfisher in 2002
This edition published in 2004
2 4 6 8 10 9 7 5 3 1
1TR/0104/TWP/GRS(GRS)/115SEM

Text copyright © Anthony Masters 2002
Illustrations copyright © Chris Fisher 2002

LIBRARY OF CONGRESS CATALOGING-IN-PUBLICATION DATA
has been applied for.

ISBN 0-7534-5800-4

Printed in India

Contents

Chapter One
Sugar Mountain

"We're going to have a treat,"
said Mel Mouse to his best friend,
Max. "Look!"
Someone had spilled a pile
of sugar on the stockroom
floor.

The sugar looked like a
big white mountain.
"You stand guard.
I'll get Molly,"
said Max.

Max ran out into the supermarket.

It was late at night.

During the day the store was

dangerous for mice.

There were people

pushing carts,

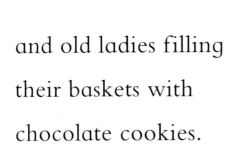

children playing

games,

and old ladies filling

their baskets with

chocolate cookies.

But at night it was

even worse.

A security guard and his

dog kept watch in the store.

The mice felt safer in the stockroom.

But Max knew Molly was in the store.

He ran to the fruit section.

Molly was nibbling on an apple.

"We've got a treat," said Max, grinning.

"Come and see."

The three mice gazed
up at the sugar mountain.
"Let's chow down!" said
Molly. She was always hungry.
"We'll eat till we're sick!"
squeaked Mel.

Then suddenly a voice snarled,
"Get your dirty paws off that sugar.
It's ours."

Max was the first
to turn around.
He didn't like
what he saw.

Then Mel and Molly turned around.
They didn't like what they saw either.

Ricky Rat and his brother,

Ronnie, had squeezed under

the door of the stockroom.

Ricky's gang was close behind.

The rats wore dark glasses.

The rats were gangsters.

They often raided the supermarket

at night.

Too often.

Ricky Rat held up a great big

water balloon.

"Back off the sugar," he said.

"Or I'll squirt you silly!"

"It's not fair," said Molly Mouse,

her paws in the air. "It's mice only

in this stockroom. We got here first."

"There isn't room for rats *and* mice in this supermarket," said Ricky.

"We're taking over," said Ronnie.

"This is *our* stockroom now."

Ricky threw the water balloon.

SPLAT!

Squeaking with fury, Mel, Max, and Molly ran away into the supermarket.

"We'll get you for this!" yelled Max.

But the rats weren't listening.

They were eating the sugar.

Chapter Two
Rat Attack

The mice ran across the floor of the

supermarket.

They were on the lookout for danger.

They were scared of the rats and

their big water balloons.

But they were also scared of the

security guard and his dog, Toby.

The mice hid behind a pot of flowers.
"Those rats are not getting away
with this," squeaked Mel.
"Soon there'll be no sugar left,"
wailed Molly.
"I've got a plan . . ." began Max.
Then suddenly he saw a long tail.
"Shhh—I think there's a rat
spying on us."

$1.99

Ronnie came out from behind the flowers. "Ricky says I've got to check on you," he said with a sugary grin. "If you try anything, you'll get your tails nipped off."

Now the mice were really scared.
The rats were fierce. The mice had
had battles with them before—
and they'd lost them all.

But it wasn't fair! The mice had found
the stockroom first, so it belonged to
them. It was their hiding place.
They *must* get rid of the rat gang.

Suddenly Toby the guard dog

ran out of the office.

The guard came too.

"Mice!" he yelled.

"Get them, Toby!"

The mice hid behind some cereal boxes.

Barking loudly, Toby charged.

Mel put his paws over his eyes.

So did Molly.

Max held his breath.

Then the telephone began to ring.

The guard ran back to his office . . .

and Toby ran with him.

The mice sighed with relief.

"Phew!" said Max. "That was close!"

Suddenly a jet of water
splashed down on them.
SPLAT!

"And I'm even
closer!" sneered
Ronnie Rat from
the top of a box
of cornflakes.
"So watch it!"

21

The mice were soaked.

"It's hopeless!" said Molly,

shivering. "We'll be stuck out

here forever."

"Toby will catch us if we can't get

back to the stockroom!"

wailed Mel.

"I've got a plan," said Max, and

he began to whisper . . .

Chapter Three
Rat Trap

Max, Mel, and Molly ran to the pet

food section.

They found a bag of dry dog food.

The mice looked around carefully—

but there was no sign of Ronnie,

the guard, or Toby.

With their sharp teeth the mice

made holes in the bag.

The dog food began to spill out.

The mice looked around again.

Everywhere was quiet.

"Now we need some paper cups,"

whispered Max.

24

Mel and Molly soon found a package.

They dragged it back to Max.

"This is hard work," said Mel.

"Stop talking and hurry up,"

hissed Max. He was

getting worried.

At any moment the

guard and Toby

might come

out of the

office.

The mice filled some cups with
dry dog food and carried them
carefully to the stockroom door.
Then they began to scatter
the food in a trail toward
the guard's office.
"I can't keep this up,"
complained Mel.

"Just keep going," snapped Max. "If we don't hurry, there'll be no sugar left."

"If that dog comes out," said Molly, "there'll be nothing of us left either."

At last the trail of dog food
led right up to the office door.
The door was open.
Toby was asleep in his basket.

"We'll have to wake up Toby," said
Max. "Then when he runs out of the
office, he'll eat the dog food and
follow the trail . . ."
". . . right to the stockroom,"
finished Mel happily.
He wasn't tired any longer.

"Then he'll smell a rat—or two," said Molly, grinning.

"He'll smell us if we're not careful," said Max. "You two go and hide behind those cans of baked beans. I'll wake up Toby."

"We can't leave you," said Molly
bravely.

But Mel was a bit of a coward.

"Yes, we can," he said—and

ran off as fast as he could.

Chapter Four
The Guard Dog

In the stockroom the rats were

still guzzling the sugar.

"Those mice are very quiet," said

Ricky, wiping sugar off his

dark glasses. "What's happened

to them?"

Ronnie peered under the door.

"No mice in sight. But someone's
dropped something on the floor.
Maybe it's more sugar," said
Ronnie greedily.
"We haven't finished this pile yet!"
said Ricky.

Bravely, Max Mouse crept into the
guard's office.

He squeaked loudly into Toby's ear—

and ran.

Toby smelled a mouse and bounded after him. Now he smelled dog food, too.

Max joined Molly and Mel behind the cans of beans. The three mice watched Toby anxiously.

Toby began to eat the dog food.

He ate all the way to the stockroom door.

Then he began to bark.

Inside the rat gang stopped eating.

"We're trapped," said Ronnie.

"It's those dirty mice," snapped Ricky, pulling his hat right down to his glasses.

"Mice who bark?" asked Ronnie.

"That's a dog, you fool!" said Ricky.

"Those mice must have set us up."

"So now there's no way out!" cried
Ronnie.

"But there's a way in," hissed
Ricky.

He dived into the sugar mountain.

Ronnie and the rest of the gang
followed him.

Chapter Five
Mice Rule

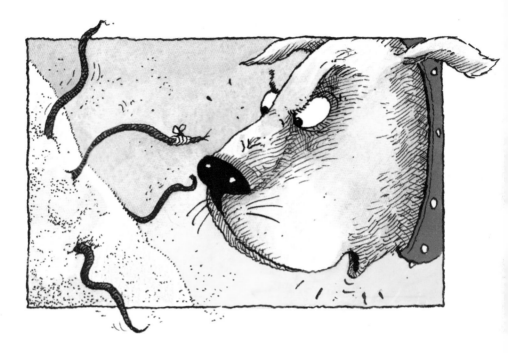

The guard pushed open the stockroom
door.

Toby dashed in, growling and barking.

The rats burrowed even deeper into the
sugar.

But their tails were still sticking out.

"Rats!" shouted the guard. "Rats in the stockroom! Get them, Toby!"

"Let's get out of here!" yelled Ricky, pulling himself out of the sugar mountain.

Ronnie and the gang were close behind him.

They dived between Toby's legs
and out through the open door.
Toby chased after them.

The rats ran past the shelf where the mice were hiding.

"You're finished," the mice squeaked.

"We rule the stockroom now."

The rats escaped through a hole under the back door of the supermarket.

"We'll be back!" yelled Ricky as he and the gang scampered away into the night.

The guard and Toby went back
to the office, and the door
slammed shut.

The mice jumped off the shelf
and ran to the stockroom.

There was no guard, no dog, and
no rat gang to stop them now.

There was plenty of the sugar mountain left.

As they began to eat Molly said, "You know what? Those rats will be back. They won't give up."

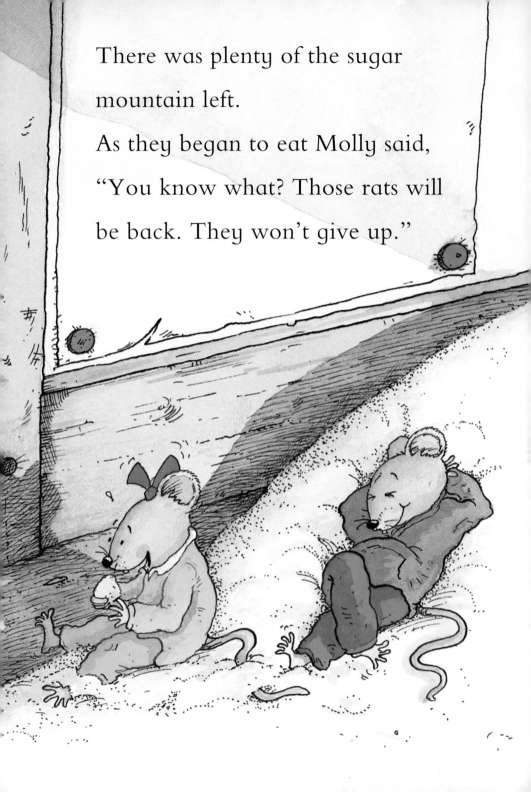

"But now that we've beaten them once, we can beat them again!" said Max.

"You bet we will," said Mel. He was feeling braver now. "Those rats are cowards. This is *our* stockroom."

"And we won't let them forget it!" said Molly.

"No," said Max. "Mice rule forever!"

About the author and illustrator

Anthony Masters used to run a children's theater and also taught drama and writing courses in schools and libraries. Anthony says, "I've often imagined what it might be like in a supermarket when it is closed at night. I think it would be a bit scary in the dark!"

Chris Fisher's favorite subject at school was art, and now he is the illustrator of more than 60 books for children. He loved drawing all the characters in the story and imagining their adventures in the supermarket. He says, "I wonder if there are any mice in my local supermarket—and whether they are as brave as Max and his friends!"

Strategies for Beginner Readers

Predict
Think about the cover, illustrations, and the title of the book. What do you think this book will be about? While you are reading think about what may happen next and why.

Monitor
As you read ask yourself if what you're reading makes sense. If it doesn't, reread, look at the illustrations, or read ahead.

Question
Ask yourself questions about important ideas in the story such as what the characters might do or what you might learn.

Phonics
If there is a word that you do not know, look carefully at the letters, sounds, and word parts that you do know. Blend the sounds to read the word. Ask yourself if this is a word you know. Does it make sense in the sentence?

Summarize
Think about the characters, the setting where the story takes place, and the problem the characters faced in the story. Tell the important ideas in the beginning, middle, and end of the story.

Evaluate
Ask yourself questions like: Did you like the story? Why or why not? How did the author make the story come alive? How did the author make the story fun to read? How well did you understand the story? Maybe you can understand it better if you read it again!